Ten Delicious Teachers

Ross Montgomery   Sarah Warburton

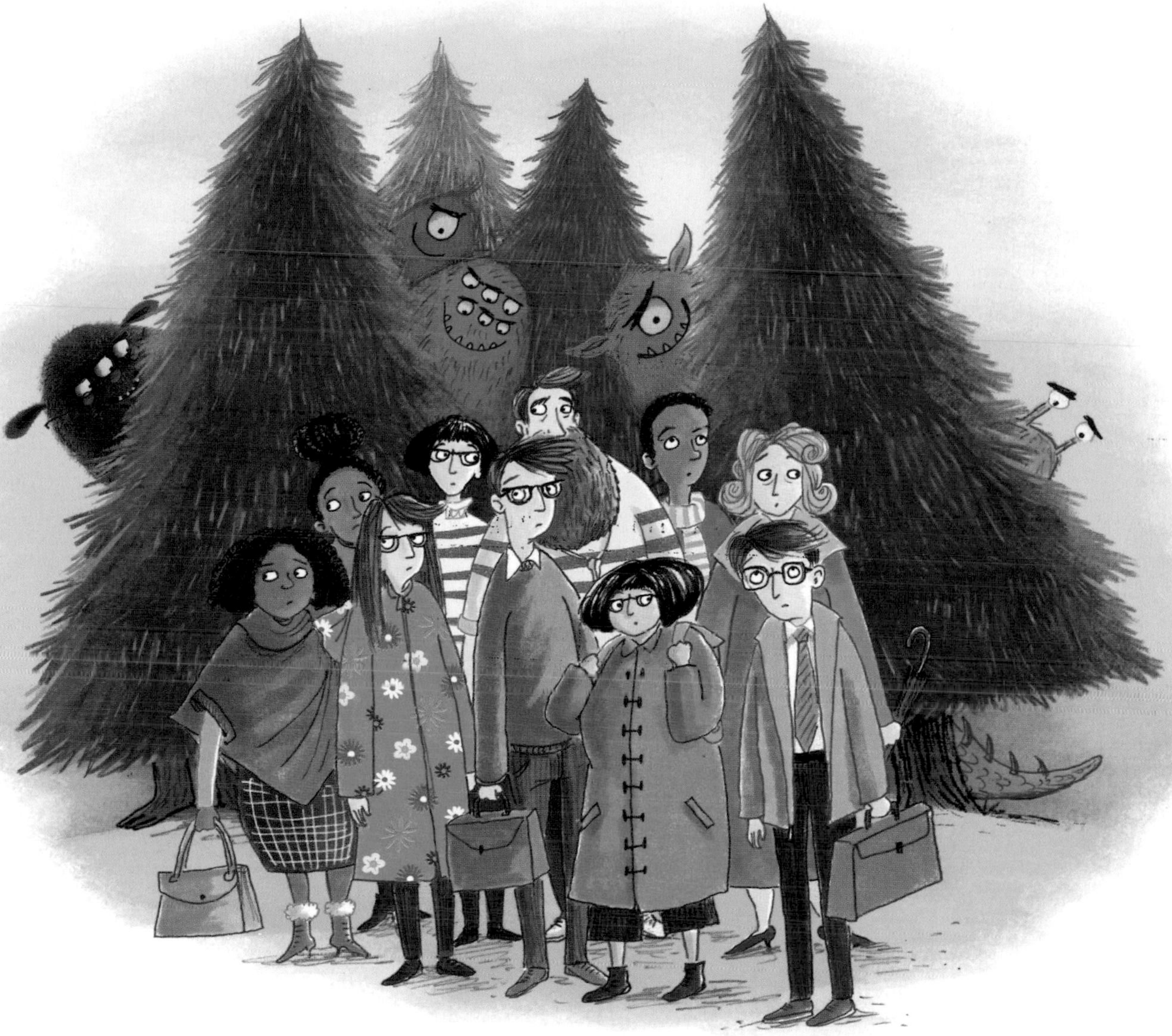

Walker Books
AND SUBSIDIARIES

LONDON · BOSTON · SYDNEY · AUCKLAND

For Charlie, aka Mr Mackinnon — watch your back. **R. M.**

To my stoic Mum, Vera, who died before I finished this book.
Gladly, not eaten by a monster (she would never have let them).
We miss you more with each passing day. **S. W.**

Ten tired teachers are finished for the day,

The kids have gone, the homework's marked, the chairs are tucked away.

They stagger through the playground with a weary, bleary groan...

Just in time to see they've missed the **last bus home!**

"Never mind," says Mr Smith. "Look at what I see —
A shortcut through the forest! We'll be home in time for tea!"

Ten foolish teachers, already celebrating,
Unaware that in the woods a monster pack is waiting...
Ten furry fiends! Ten bristly brutes! Ten hairy hungry beasts
Are hidden in the trees to have themselves a teacher feast.

Ten delicious teachers, skipping through the trees,
Surrounded by a paradise of plants and bugs and bees.
Mrs Dawlish stops to pause and pick a dandelion...
A monster creeps up right behind her!

Now there's only...

Nine delicious teachers, hiking up the path,
Tailed by a naughty monster trying not to laugh.

Mr Fenton falls behind and now is running late...
He stops to rest and catch his breath!

Now **there's only...**

Eight delicious teachers, walking in a line,

Hopping over stepping stones a teacher at a time.

Miss McKenzie doesn't stop to see where she is heading...

Straight into the monster's mouth!

Now **there's only...**

Seven delicious teachers, strolling down the lane,
Wondering how long it is until they're home again.
But wait — what's this beside the path?
A kind and thoughtful gift...

WORLD'S BEST TEACHER

Madame Masson falls for it!

Now **there's only...**

Six delicious teachers, stalking through the grass,

Singing songs and waving sticks and marching extra fast.

Mr Kendall doesn't see the hidden gleaming eyes...

The monsters have surrounded him!

Now there's only...

Five delicious teachers, their journey nearly done,
Wondering why half the staff have vanished one by one.
They row across a scenic lake to reach the sandy shore...

Mr Meadows doesn't make it!

Now **there's only...**

Four delicious teachers on a creaky wooden bridge,

Taking careful steps to reach the fearsome rocky ridge.

No one sees the beast above them, swooping from the trees...

To snaffle Mrs Fortunata!

Now **there's only...**

Wobbly rope Bridge

Three delicious teachers, feeling bold and brave,
Sneaking through the darkness of a cold and creepy cave.
Mrs Joseph takes a break — a foolish thing to do...
She lights a match to find her way!

Now there's only...

TWO delicious teachers, the only pair remaining,

They're cold and lost, it's getting dark — it's even started raining!

Mr Smith's determined for the journey to be done...

He goes to read the helpful map!

Now there's **only**...

One delicious teacher left – in fact, a nursery teacher,
Used to dealing with all kinds of noisy, smelly creatures.
Miss Hunter is her name, and now the monster pack has found her.
They rub their hands and lick their lips and quickly close around her...

"Stop that at once!"

Miss Hunter shouts.

The beasts are stopped completely.

"You naughty things!" Miss Hunter cries.

"How dare you try to eat me?

Who taught you to behave this way?

What's that? No explanation?

I think it's time you beasts received a proper education..."

Ten uneasy monsters at their brand-new monster school,

Learning how to be polite and follow all the rules:

"Don't eat your desk!

Say 'please' and 'thanks'!

And never bite your friends!

Now get your books, today we'll learn the numbers one to ten..."

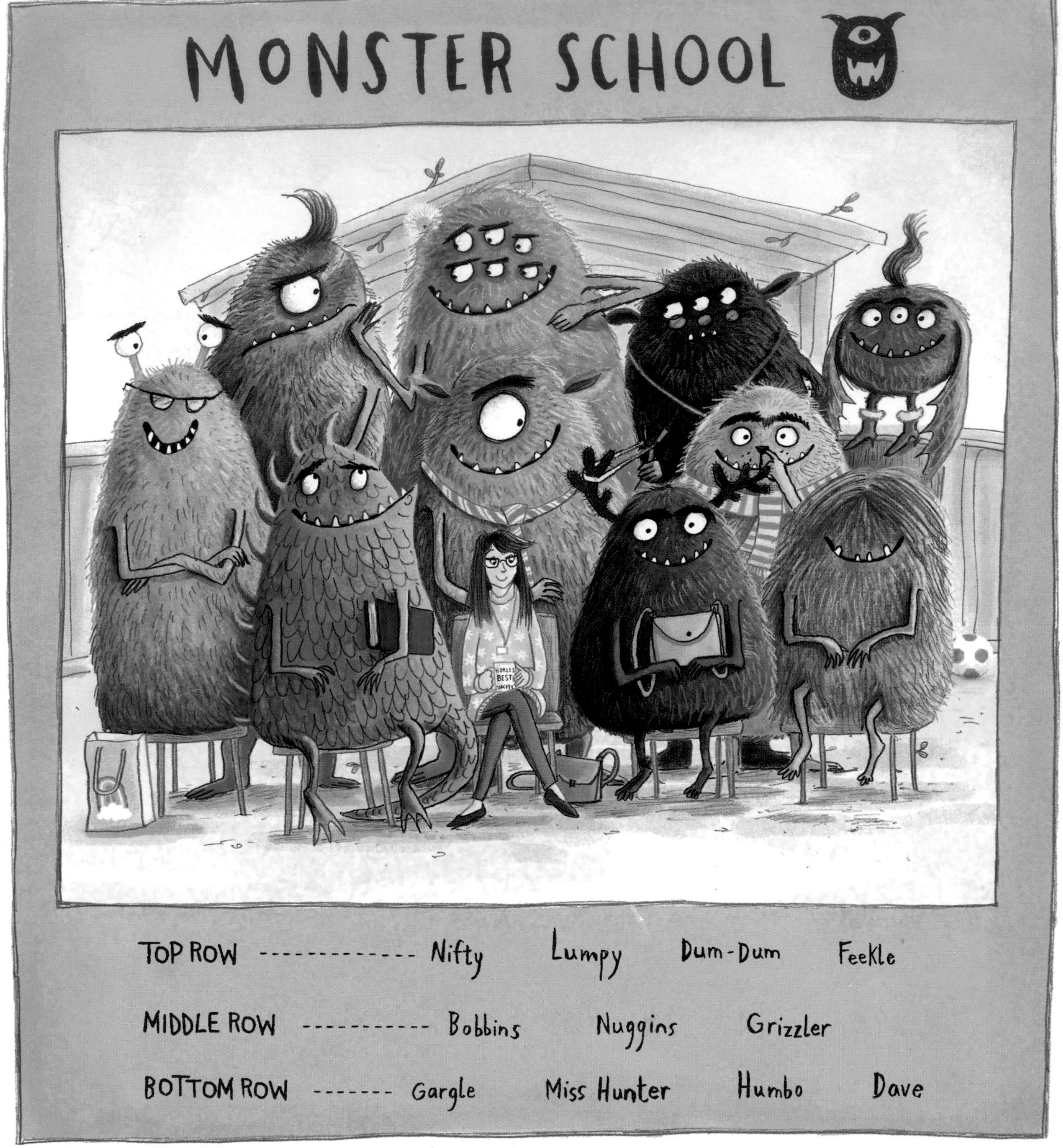

MONSTER SCHOOL

TOP ROW ------------- Nifty   Lumpy   Dum-Dum   Feekle

MIDDLE ROW ----------- Bobbins   Nuggins   Grizzler

BOTTOM ROW ------- Gargle   Miss Hunter   Humbo   Dave